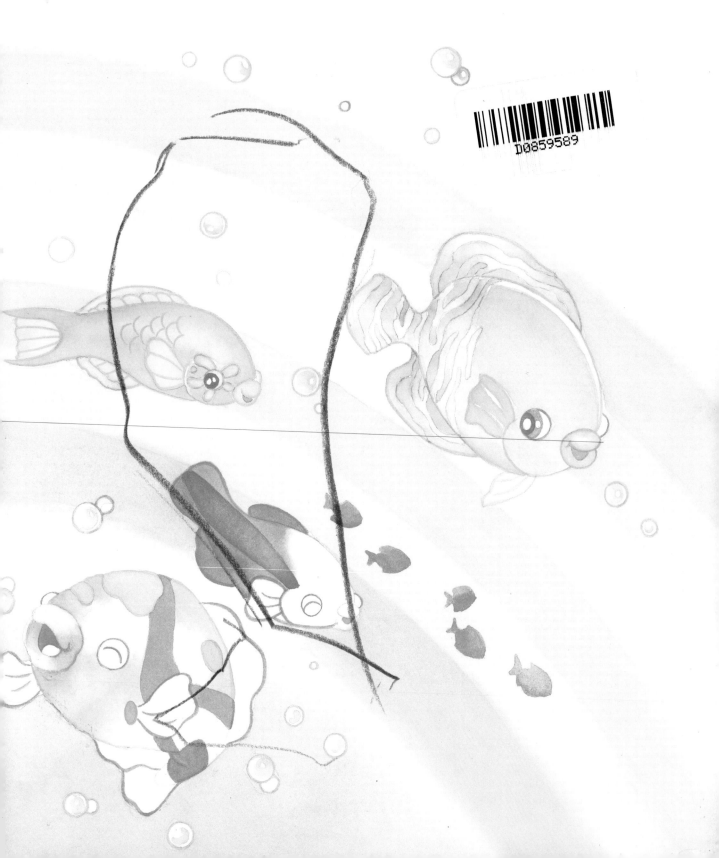

Published by

ISLAND HERITAGE™
P U B L I S H I N G

A DIVISION OF THE MADDEN CORPORATION

94-411 KŌ'AKI STREET, WAIPAHU, HAWAI'I 96797-2806
PHONE: (800) 468-2800 • FAX : (800) 564-8877
islandheritage.com

ISBN# 1-59700-243-7

First Edition, Second Printing – 2007

Humu's Search for a Rainbow

Written by Kimberly A. Jackson   **Illustrated by Yuko Green**

To Greg and Keli
Kimberly

For Waikoloa Baptist Keikiland children who showed me a colorful rainbow
Aunty Yuko

Humuhumunukunukuāpuaʻa was basking in the rays of sun hitting the ocean when he spotted a familiar sight.

"Look, everyone," Humu called to his friends.
"Turtle has returned!"

2

"Tell us what you've seen,"
Humu said to Turtle.

The other fishes swished their tails excitedly.
They all loved to hear about Turtle's adventures
in that mysterious, faraway place called land.

3

"I saw an arc of colors in the sky above land—all the colors you can imagine," Turtle told the fishes. "It's called a rainbow, and it's the most beautiful sight in the world."

"Land sounds much more exciting than our home," Humu said. "I wish the ocean had rainbows."

"Me, too," replied Tang, a shiny yellow fish who was also Humu's best friend.

"The ocean is boring," said a sparkly blue fish.

Humu pouted. "I'm going to hide in a cave and try to forget about rainbows."

5

Turtle floated
lazily on his back.
"Do as you wish, Humu.
But no matter where you go,
you'll never get to see a rainbow
like I did."

Humu swam off toward his favorite hiding place.

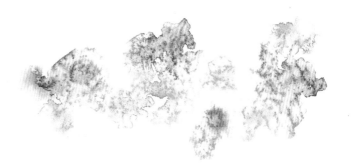

As he swam, he spotted colors shimmering in the distance. "Could that be a rainbow?" Humu said. "I'm going to get a closer look."

"There are no rainbows in the ocean," said Turtle.

"Maybe," said Humu, "but I want to see for myself."

"Be careful," said a glowing green fish. "This ocean can be dangerous."

Humu swam toward the colors—red and orange, yellow and green, blue and violet—without paying attention to where he was swimming.

Suddenly Humu couldn't see anything. He trembled as he realized he was in a deep ocean trench. Unless he escaped quickly, he'd be lunch for a giant fish lurking nearby.

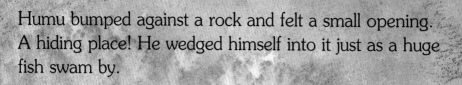

Humu bumped against a rock and felt a small opening.
A hiding place! He wedged himself into it just as a huge
fish swam by.

"I wish I could visit land and see a rainbow," Humu thought.
But he knew he never would. He also knew he couldn't stay
in this rock forever. He had to get back home.

12

"Swim!" he told himself as he darted out of his hiding place. "Swim as fast as you can!"

As Humu swam he spied shimmering colors. This time, however, they seemed to be chasing him.

Humu was scared. He hurried away from the colors and worried he'd never reach the safety of the coral reef.

Just then, he noticed bubbles
up ahead. Lots and lots
of bubbles. Perhaps they were
coming from a friendly whale.

Humu swam toward the bubbles.

When he was surrounded by them...

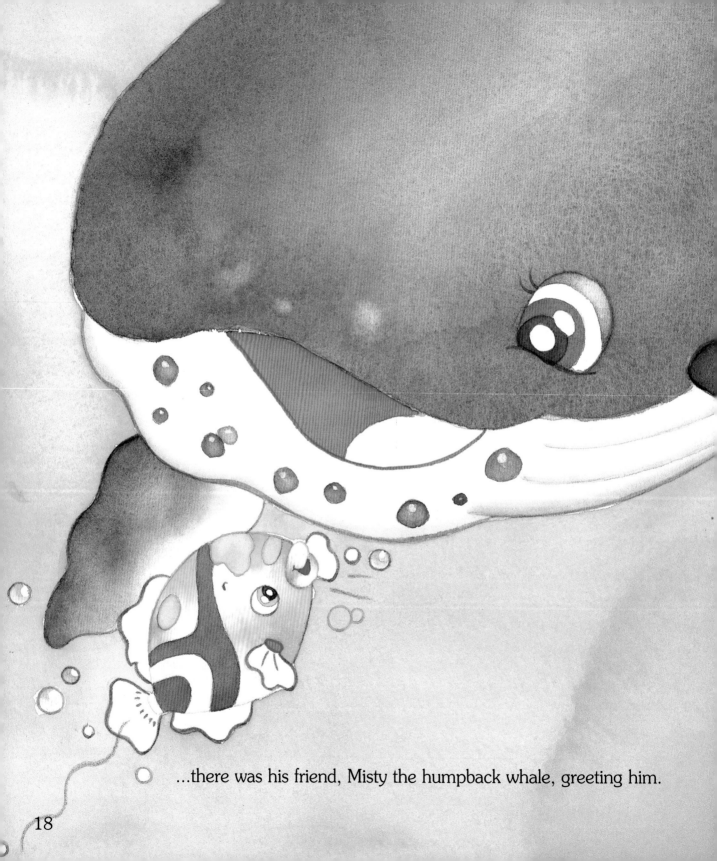

...there was his friend, Misty the humpback whale, greeting him.

18

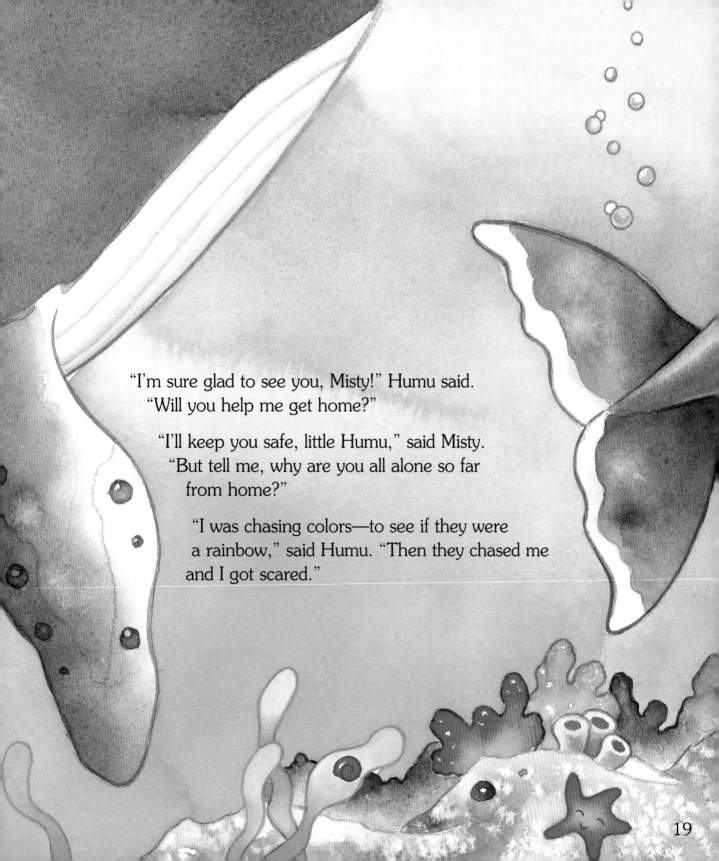

"I'm sure glad to see you, Misty!" Humu said.
"Will you help me get home?"

"I'll keep you safe, little Humu," said Misty.
"But tell me, why are you all alone so far
from home?"

"I was chasing colors—to see if they were
a rainbow," said Humu. "Then they chased me
and I got scared."

19

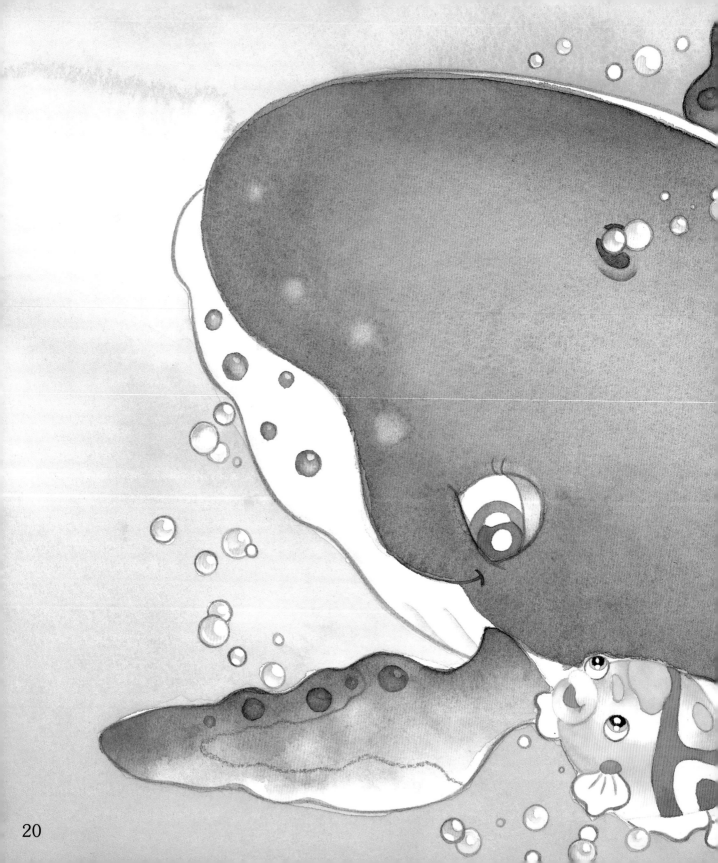

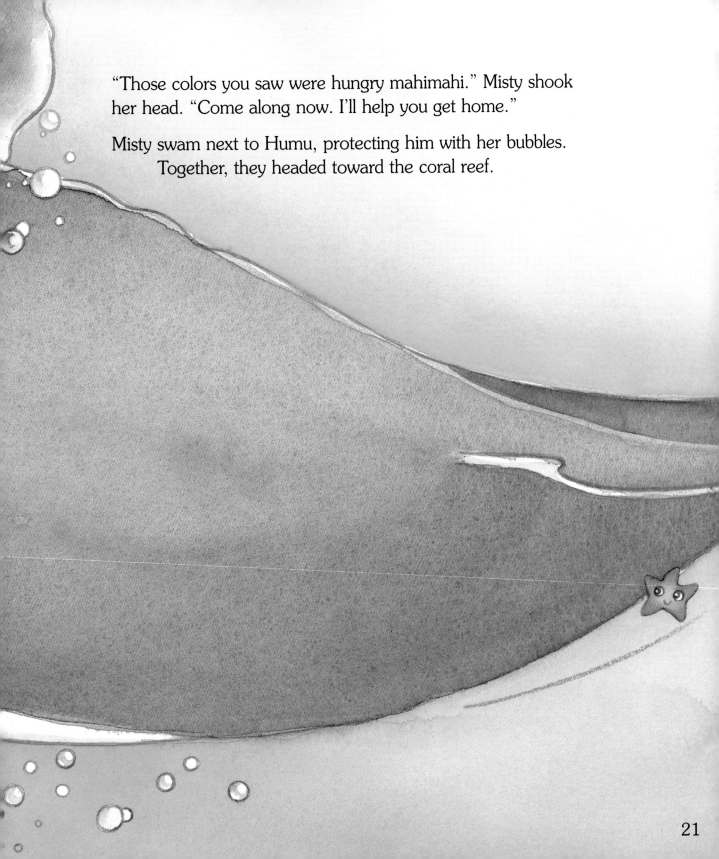

"Those colors you saw were hungry mahimahi." Misty shook her head. "Come along now. I'll help you get home."

Misty swam next to Humu, protecting him with her bubbles. Together, they headed toward the coral reef.

"I'll never see a rainbow," Humu thought sadly.

As Humu neared the reef, he again saw colors—a patch
of green, a smear of yellow, a smudge of red. He knew
now that they couldn't be a rainbow. If those colors were
mahimahi, his fish friends would be in danger. He was glad
Misty was there to keep them safe.

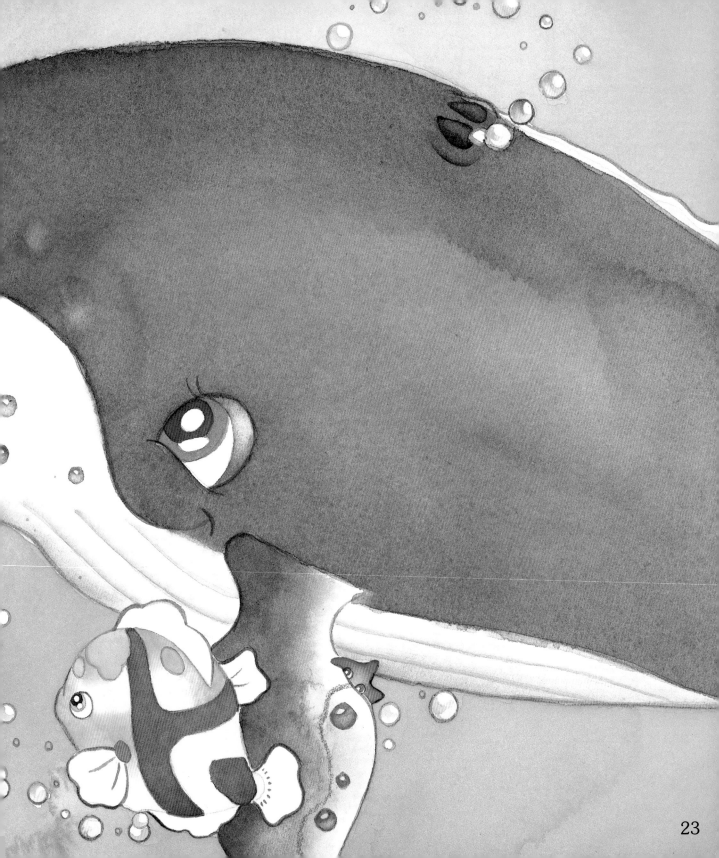

When Humu got closer to the colors he could see they were his fish friends, feeding on the reef. Red and orange fish, yellow and green fish, blue and violet fish.

"You're home now," said Misty.
"It's time for me to say goodbye."
　　She slapped her tail on the water,
　　then sped away.

　　Humu rushed to the reef.

"We're so glad you're home!" said his best friend Tang.

"Me, too!" Humu said. "And just wait until Turtle comes back. I'm going to tell him he was wrong."

"What do you mean?" asked a sparkly blue fish.

All the reef fish gathered to hear Humu's answer.

"Look around," said Humu.

Humu's fish friends looked around.

"My friends, we don't have to go to land to see a rainbow because," Humu said, "we do have beautiful rainbows right here in the ocean."

"What? Rainbows?" said a glowing green fish.

"Yes," said Humu, looking wise.
"Fish rainbows!"

GLOSSARY

Bigeyes (Āweoweo)

Angelfish

Yellow Tang (Lauʻīpala)

Sunset Wrasse

Eyestriped Surgeonfish
(Palani)

Hawaiian Cleaner Wrasse

Reef Triggerfish
(Humuhumunukunukuāpuaʻa)

Green Sea Turtle (Honu)

Bluefin Trevally/Blue Jack (ʻŌmilu)

31

THE END